THIS BOOK BELONGS TO:

OTHER MY FRIEND PARIS BOOKS

Published by:

New Year Publishing, LLC   144 Diablo Ranch Ct.   Danville, CA 94506 USA

orders@newyearpublishing.com   http://www.newyearpublishing.com

Library of Congress Control Number: 2011943977

ISBN:978-1-61431-053-2

NEW YEAR
PUBLISHING, LLC.

My Twins' First Christmas

by Jackie Singer

Thank you to Dave and Paris for making this all possible. Thank you Mom and Dad for all of your help, and thank you to my little sister Kate for giving me the life experience to be able to write this story. — Jackie

My name is Paris. I have twin sisters, Liberty & Victoria, and this December is my twins' first Christmas. I'm so excited to teach them our family traditions!

Early in December, our whole family drives to the tree farm to pick out a Christmas tree. I love the smell of the pine trees and finding the perfect tree. It's really cold out, so I hope it snows soon!

The twins seem to have more
fun playing hide & seek.

When we get home, we decorate the tree. Everyone has a special ornament and this year, we have two new ones!

The only problem is that the twins are pulling the ornaments off! We don't want them to break any, so we have to put a fence around the tree.

Daddy does a great job putting up pretty lights on our house. We bundle up in our hats & mittens and walk around the neighborhood looking at everyone else's decorations too. Some people decorate with fake snow, but I'm keeping my fingers crossed that real snow falls. Daddy says that it's possible, but it doesn't snow very often where we live.

Every year, we go to my friend Lincoln's house when they celebrate Hanukkah. Some Jewish families serve potato latkes, but in Israel they eat jelly doughnuts. The doughnuts Lincoln's Grandma makes are delicious!

This year, they let me light their menorah candles and then we showed Liberty & Victoria how to spin the dreidels.

In preschool, I learn that not everyone celebrates Christmas or Hanukkah. Some people celebrate Kwanzaa, which means 'first fruits of the harvest' in Swahili. Kwanzaa is a weeklong celebration honoring African—American heritage and culture.

One of my favorite traditions is walking around Union Square and looking at all of the shop window displays. We make a list and shop for the perfect gifts to give everyone. The twins like the huge display of stuffed animals in the toy store the best.

Today I get to go ice skating with my friends Jackie & Lincoln. I want to teach the twins how to ice skate, but Mommy says they just learned how to walk and are not ready to go ice skating yet.

While we are shopping, Mommy and Daddy take us to see Santa. I have been a really good girl this year, and I'm sure Santa will get me what I ask for. I also tell him what I think the twins would like. My special request is that it will snow on Christmas.

Liberty keeps trying to pull Santa's glasses
off again and again. Victoria isn't so sure
about Santa and starts to cry.

The twins and I bake cookies with Grandma Linda to give to our neighbors. Liberty and Victoria make a mess with the icing and like to play with the dough.

Mommy has the idea to donate all of the extra cookies to charity. It makes me happy to see the smiles on everyone's faces.

Every year, the city where we live puts up a giant 'tree' made of just lights. It's a family tradition to look up and spin around under it.

I get dizzy, but it's lots of fun. The twins laugh and fall down a lot!

HOT CHOCOLATE

On Christmas Eve, after a big dinner with our whole family, we set out a glass of milk and cookies for Santa and some carrots for his reindeer.

Liberty and Victoria are too excited to go to sleep, so they snuggle into bed with me and Mommy reads us a Christmas story.

It's finally Christmas morning! The twins and I wake up before it's even light out. We run to the tree to see what Santa has left for us.

Santa brought the twins just what I asked for: a beautiful new doll for Liberty and Victoria got a fun toy to ride on. Mommy said I also got my special Christmas wish — when I looked outside, I saw that it had snowed overnight!

Mommy & Daddy take us to the park where we go sledding and make snow angels. It is the perfect Christmas day!

The End

For more information on Paris' adventures,
visit http://www.myfriendparis.com

Lightning Source UK Ltd.
Milton Keynes UK
UKHW05n0648061018
330077UK00005B/31/P